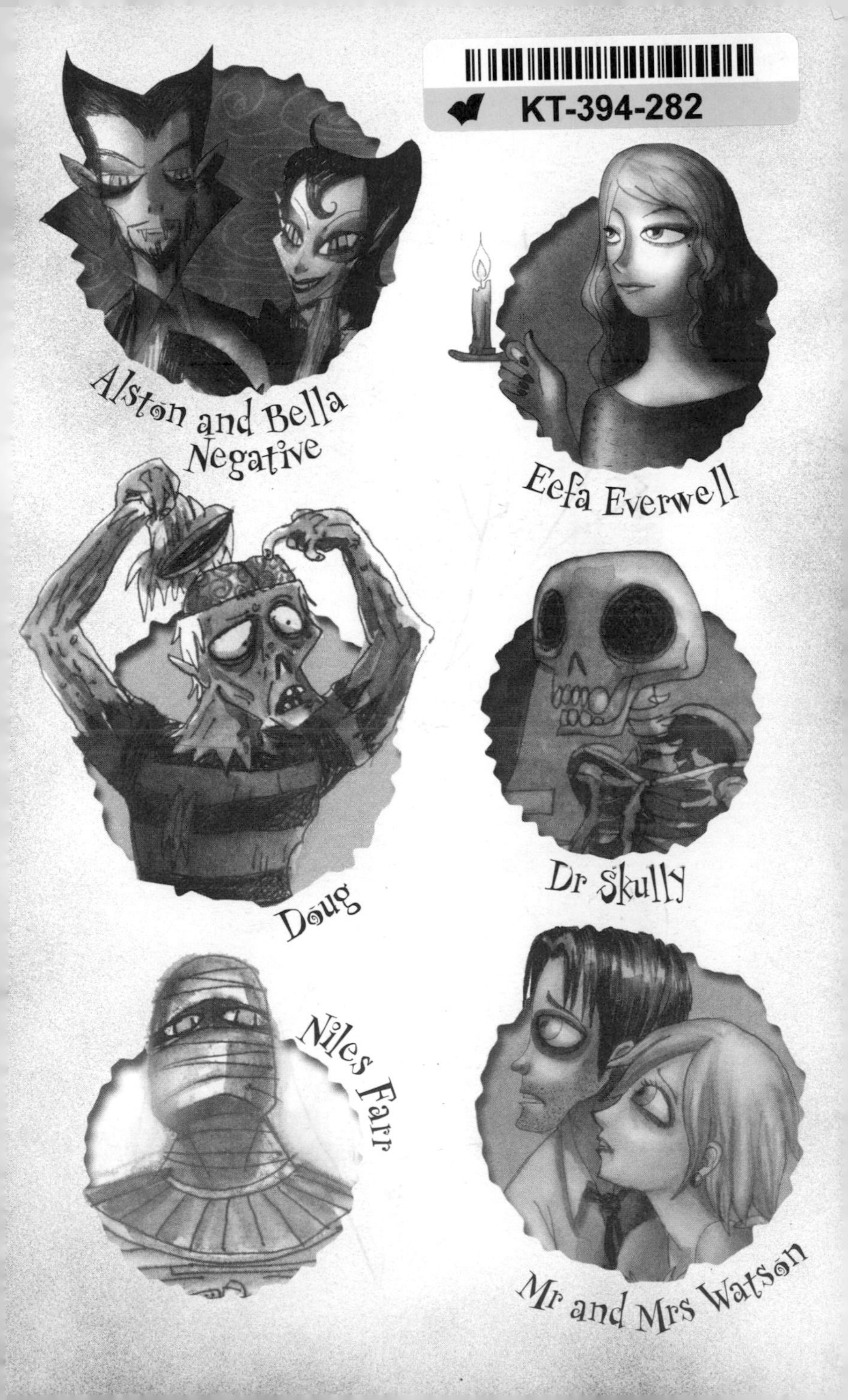
KT-394-282
Alston and Bella
Negative
Eefa Everwell
Doug
Dr Skully
Niles Farr
Mr and Mrs Watson

Welcome to Scream Street
D
E
G
I
L
J
M
N
F
B
K
O
G
H
A
P

Meet the residents...
Luke Watson
Cleo Farr
Resus Negative
Dixon
Sir Otto Sneer
Samuel Skipstone

For my sister, Sue,
with apologies for forcing our parents to
change your name from Jayne to Susan when you
first came home from hospital!

Who lives where...

- A Sneer Hall
- B Central square
- C Everwell's Emporium
- D No. 2: The Crudleys
- E No. 5: The Movers
- F No. 11: Twinkle
- G No. 13: Luke Watson
- H No. 14: Resus Negative
- I No. 21: Eefa Everwell
- J No. 22: Cleo Farr
- K No. 26: The Headless Horseman
- L No. 27: Femur Ribs
- M No. 28: Doug, Turf and Berry
- N No. 31: Kian Negative
- O No. 32: Ryan Aire
- P No. 39: The Skullys

Previously on Scream Street...

Mr and Mrs Watson were terrified when their son, Luke, first transformed into a werewolf. But that was nothing compared to their terror at being forcibly moved to Scream Street – and discovering there was no going back.

Determined to take his parents home, Luke enlisted the help of his new friends, Resus Negative, a wannabe vampire, and Cleo Farr, an Egyptian mummy, to find six relics left behind by the community's founding fathers. Only by collecting these magical artefacts would he be able to open a doorway back to his own world.

Just as Luke and his friends finally succeeded in their quest, Mr and Mrs Watson realized how happy Luke had become in his new home and decided to stay on in Scream Street. But the newly opened doorway was becoming a problem – Sir Otto Sneer, the street's wicked landlord, was charging "normals" from Luke's world to visit what he called "the world's greatest freak show".

To protect Scream Street, Luke, Resus and Cleo must try to close the doorway by returning the relics to their original owners – and this time their quest involves precious gemstones, a terrible curse ... and some very bad smells.

Chapter One
The Attic

The faceless men stumbled like robots across the lawn towards the front of the house. Smooth, blank skin covered where their eyes, noses and mouths should have been. Each figure was dressed in a shiny purple jumpsuit with "G.H.O.U.L." printed on the back.

There was a slight shimmer in the air, then the ghost of a young boy materialized among the men. He studied them closely as they shambled towards the house.

"*Psst!* Over here!" The voice was coming from a large bush in the middle of the front lawn. The ghost hovered towards it cautiously. "Er … hello?"

A pale face appeared among the leaves, a tongue licking nervously over small fangs. "Get in here!" Resus Negative ordered.

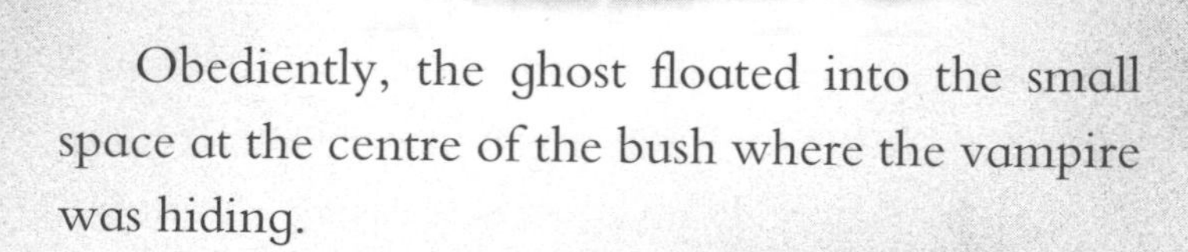

Obediently, the ghost floated into the small space at the centre of the bush where the vampire was hiding.

"What's going on?" he asked, intrigued.

"You tell me," replied Resus. "We've been watching this house for days – ever since the Spectre family moved away. I've got cramp in muscles I never knew I had!"

"Why?"

"Probably because I've been stuck in this bush since eight o'clock this mor—"

"No," said the ghost, "why have you been watching the house?"

"So that we'd know when someone else moved in," said Resus. "We needed to work out when the Movers would be busy so…" He paused, pushing a leafy branch to one side and allowing daylight to fall across the ghost's face. "Hang on, I know you, don't I?"

The ghost nodded. "My name's Ryan," he said. "Ryan Aire. You helped to rescue me after I'd been kidnapped by the Nightwatchman."

Resus winced at the memory. The Nightwatchman had been a dark, evil creature who terrorized sleeping children. The young vampire and his friends had very nearly died in his clutches. "What are you doing here?" he asked.

"We're the ones moving in," said Ryan with a smile. "When I returned home after you rescued me, I told my family all about you – the three brave kids from Scream Street. My dad said it was the sort of place we should live, so he asked G.H.O.U.L. to move us."

Resus couldn't resist a grin. "Three brave kids, eh?" he said. "You know, *I* was the one who did most of the rescuing. The other two just followed my— *Aargh!*"

One of the Movers had pulled Resus out of the bush and clamped a hand to his forehead. A voice echoed through the vampire's mind: "Where do the CDs go?"

Resus pulled the hand away crossly. "I've no idea where the CDs go!" he exclaimed. "This isn't my stuff."

"Those are my mum's CDs," said Ryan, melting out of the bush. "I can show him where she keeps them. You can come too if you like..."

But Resus was already hurrying across the lawn. "Another time," he called back over his shoulder. "Right now I've got some news to pass on!" He leapt the garden fence and raced away.

"I *knew* it wouldn't be long before the Movers had a job on," said Resus as he crossed Scream Street's central square with his friends, Luke Watson and Cleo Farr. "This is our chance."

"Did Ryan say where the Spectres had moved to?" asked Cleo.

"I didn't ask," admitted Resus. "I left straight away to get you two. What matters is that with the Movers out of the way we can get up into their attic and give Heru back his relic!"

He pulled an ancient, mummified heart from under his cape. The organ, wrapped in bandages, was the third of six relics the trio had collected in order to open a doorway back to Luke's world. However, they now had to return it to its original donor to close the portal and rid the community of invading tourists.

A thin, ginger-haired man stood by the multi-coloured doorway in the middle of the square. He gave the trio a cheery wave, then turned to collect money from another group of normals as they stepped through into Scream Street.

"Look," said Cleo with glee. "They're having to stoop to get in!" Luke and Resus watched as a particularly tall man bent down to fit through.

The doorway had originally been made up of six different-coloured bands of light, but each time the trio returned one of the founding fathers' relics, one of the stripes in the arch disappeared. With two relics already returned, only four colours remained: yellow, purple, green and orange. And the doorway was definitely shrinking.

"They'll be crawling in on their hands and knees before long," grinned Resus.

"Not soon enough for my liking," said Luke with a sigh as he watched the group of normals beginning to explore the square. "Come on..."

The trio dodged through the crowds until

they reached the Movers' own house, number 5. Resus was about to slide one of his fake finger-nails into the lock on the front door when Cleo stopped him.

"Try this," she suggested, handing him a small object. Luke looked at it over Resus's shoulder and saw what appeared to be finger bones.

Resus stared in astonishment. "A skeleton key!" he exclaimed. "I've never seen one in real life. Where on earth did you get it?"

"Back when we were still in Egypt, a couple of explorers broke into my tomb," Cleo explained. "They were going to use this to open my sarcophagus before my dad burst in and scared them off. They dropped it as they fled."

"Can it open anything?" asked Luke.

Cleo shrugged. "I've never used it before."

"Hang on," said Resus. "If you've had a skeleton key all this time, why have I been risking my nails in every locked door and window we've come across?"

"I'd forgotten all about it until last night," said Cleo. "I found it in an old jewellery box when I was tidying my room."

"Typical," scowled Resus. "What else have

you got stashed away in your room that we could have used? A banshee silencer? A set of rat pulverizers?"

Luke snatched the key from Resus impatiently. "Are we going to use this, or argue about it?" He slipped it into the lock. At first it seemed too small, but slowly the bones began to move, expanding and realigning until they fitted perfectly.

The key then turned of its own accord and the door swung open. Luke quickly ushered his friends inside and Cleo closed the door behind them, plunging the house into blackness. The trio crept tentatively along the silent hallway.

"I don't know why the Movers insist on living in the dark," said Resus, pulling a flaming torch from his cloak.

"They're blind," Cleo reminded him. "Why would they need lights?"

Resus shrugged. "We can't be the first people ever to visit them."

"By 'visiting them', I assume you mean 'breaking in'?" said Luke. "That's what we're doing, remember – so keep your voices down!"

The vampire led the way, keeping a look-out in case one of the Movers had decided to take a

day off and stay at home.

At the top of the stairs, they stopped at the foot of a ladder leading up to the attic.

"This is it," said Luke. "Just remember to watch out for the spiders."

Cleo shuddered. The last time the three children had entered this attic, they had become trapped in thick webbing and almost been smothered by the thousands of tiny black spiders that had been placed around Heru's sarcophagus to guard it.

Resus gripped the handle of his torch. "The spiders hate fire, remember?" he said. "Leave them to me. I'll be right behind you."

Luke began to climb the ladder. When he reached the top, he slid back the bolt and pushed open the trapdoor in the ceiling before climbing through it into the attic.

Cleo and Resus clambered after him and the three of them stood silently for a moment.

"The spiders..." said Cleo, cocking her head to one side. "I can't hear them."

"Me neither," agreed Luke. "The webs are still here, though."

Resus held the torch out at arm's length.

Swathes of dull, grey gossamer hung limply from the roof beams. "It's all dried out!" he exclaimed.

"I don't like the look of this," Luke admitted.

"So, the spiders have gone," said Cleo. "That's a good thing, isn't it?"

Resus shrugged. "I suppose so," he said. "It means we won't have to fight our way past them to get to Heru."

"I'm not worried about the spiders," said Luke. "But what's Heru doing without anything to protect his sarcophagus?"

"Maybe he didn't need them once he gave you his relic?" suggested Cleo.

"Maybe," Luke replied, unconvinced. "Let's find him as quick as we can, give the heart back and get out of here."

Luke felt more of the dry gossamer brush against his cheek as he pressed on across the attic, the others close behind. The old webbing deadened the sound of their footsteps, and he could hear his own heartbeat thumping loudly in his ears. Then he saw a movement in the shadows ahead.

He could just make out a figure in the gloom, seated by the furthest wall. "Heru?" he whispered.

"We've got something for you..."

"I'm afraid Heru doesn't live here any more," growled a deep voice.

A lump caught in Luke's throat and he squinted at the speaker in the dim light. It couldn't be...

But it was. Sitting in an armchair in the exact spot where Heru's sarcophagus should have been was Scream Street's landlord, Sir Otto Sneer.

Chapter Two
The Mouse

"What are *you* doing here?" Luke asked incredulously.

Sir Otto bit down on his cigar. "You were expecting someone else?" he teased.

"Where's Heru?" Cleo demanded. "What have you done with him?"

The landlord pulled a mock-innocent face. "*Done* with him?" he asked. "I really don't know what you're talking about..."

"Don't play games with us!" snapped Resus.

"Or what?" demanded the landlord, jumping to his feet. "Do you really think three kids can get one over on me?"

"The doorway to my world is shrinking, Sneer," said Luke. "We've already returned two of the founding fathers' relics..."

Sir Otto blew a cloud of noxious cigar smoke into Luke's face. "And that's where it stops, boy," he snarled. "You might have won a battle or two, but it is I who shall prevail in the war!" He smoothed a crease from the white silk scarf tied around his neck. "After all – how can you give Heru back his heart if he's not here?"

"We'll find him," Luke assured the landlord. "Just you watch!"

A mouse scuttled in front of them, its whiskers twitching.

"Blasted mice everywhere!" bellowed Sir Otto, swinging his leg and kicking the rodent across the attic floor.

Cleo hurried over to where it had slammed

into the wall. "You monster!" she cried, collecting up the dazed mouse and cradling it in her palm.

Sir Otto spat out the butt of his cigar and crushed it with his boot. Pulling a fresh one from his pocket, he leant in to Resus to light it from the flaming torch. "This has been fun," he rumbled. "I'd love it if we could get together like this more often. But I'm afraid that's not going to be possible..."

As he finished speaking, three Movers stepped out of the darkness behind the children. The landlord touched his fingers to the forehead of the one standing closest to him. "Take them downstairs," he instructed.

Luke struggled as the Mover secured the final leather restraint around his wrist. He, Resus and Cleo were all strapped into chairs in the Movers' kitchen, their hands, feet and necks securely bound.

Sir Otto entered carrying the flaming torch. "You might have wondered why the Movers have no facial features," he growled. "The reason is this: if they cannot see, hear, taste or smell, they can never accidentally reveal the true location of G.H.O.U.L.'s communities."

"How interesting," said Luke sarcastically. "Have you ever considered taking over from Dr Skully?"

Sir Otto ignored the remark and wedged the torch behind the door handle. "Contrary to popular belief," he continued, "Movers are not born as obedient robots. They start out just like you or me – well, me anyway – and have their senses removed manually."

"You mean they're *human*?" Cleo gasped, struggling to turn her head and look up at the smooth-skinned face of the Mover beside her.

"They're more than just human," replied the landlord. "They're normals. Usually the meddlesome type who stick their noses into vampire sightings and rumours of zombies. The type who ask too many questions. Occasionally one of them discovers the existence of a place such as Scream Street, and then G.H.O.U.L. is forced to, shall we say … take them out of the picture."

"They're turned into Movers against their will?" cried Resus. "That's barbaric!"

"It is indeed," Sir Otto agreed. "I could be charging those same normals to come in and look around!"

"You're despicable," growled Luke as his straps were tightened.

"Yes," beamed the landlord, "I am, aren't I? I have told the Movers that you are to be recruited to the cause. Your eyes, noses, ears and mouths will be removed and replaced with skin from your backs."

Cleo whimpered softly and shrank back in her chair.

Sir Otto leant down to give her a malicious smile. "I'll inform your parents that you set off on another of your little adventures and – sadly – failed to return. And the best part is that you'll never be able to tell anyone any different!"

Resus swallowed hard, his mouth dry.

Sir Otto pressed his hand against the forehead of the nearest Mover. "Begin with the werewolf," he ordered. "If he tries to transform, you'll find two more 'volunteers' at number 13 – his parents!" With a final glare at the children, he turned and marched out of the kitchen. A few seconds later they heard the front door slam behind him.

The faceless men began to root through the kitchen for makeshift tools. One of them produced an ice-cream scoop from a drawer.

"OK," gulped Resus. "This is officially bad! What do we do?"

"I don't know," admitted Luke. "I could change into my werewolf and try to fight back, but I don't dare in case they go after my mum and dad next."

"Look!" hissed Cleo as something in the shadows caught her attention. "It's the mouse from the attic – the one Sir Otto kicked."

"Brilliant," scoffed Resus. "We're about to get our eyes popped out of our heads, and all you care about is some stupid rodent."

"Just look at it!" insisted Cleo. "It's getting bigger!"

Luke winced as another of the Movers picked up a pair of rusty scissors.

"She's right!" exclaimed Resus. "The mouse is growing!"

"Oh good," said Luke. "Do let me know when it's big enough to leave home and get a nest of its own..."

"Not that kind of growing!" yelled Cleo. She watched in amazement as the creature's ears shrank back into its head and its tail widened, gradually growing into a thick flap of material.

The Movers, now with a hammer added to their toolkit, turned towards Luke.

"Think of something – fast!" he cried.

Resus was still looking at the mouse. "I don't believe it..." he croaked. A human face appeared where the mouse's nose and whiskers had been, and its soft, grey skin became a long leather coat. "It's you!"

One of the Movers raised the scissors to Luke's face and Cleo screamed.

Shakily, the figure stood, pressed his hand to the temple of the nearest Mover and barked a single word. "Stop!"

Then he collapsed to the floor.

Luke, Resus and Cleo helped Zeal Chillchase out into the Movers' back garden, where he slumped against the house, clutching at his side. It had clearly taken a supreme effort for him to stand and untie all three children.

Cleo knelt beside him. "Are you OK?" she asked. Zeal Chillchase was the Tracker who had moved Luke and his family to Scream Street, and while the children remained nervous of the powerful figure, he had proved to be a trusted

ally by promising to help them in their quest to close the doorway to Luke's world.

"I think Sir Otto broke one of my ribs when he kicked me," he wheezed. "If not for that, I'd have shapeshifted back and stopped the Movers earlier."

"Was it true what Sir Otto said?" asked Resus. "Does G.H.O.U.L. really turn nosy normals into Movers?"

Zeal Chillchase shifted to ease his discomfort. "That used to be the way they did it," he replied. "But not for decades. The Movers are immortal, so once G.H.O.U.L. had enough of them, they stopped recruiting."

"Immortal?" cried Resus. "You mean they live for ever?"

Zeal nodded. "They had to get something in return for losing four of their senses. G.H.O.U.L. obviously thought immortality was a suitable replacement."

"If you ask me, I think it's disgusting," scowled Cleo.

"I agree," said Chillchase. "But none of this gets you any closer to returning Heru's heart."

"You knew why we were up there?" asked Luke.

"I've been watching Sir Otto for the past couple of days," the Tracker explained. "I knew he was up to something when he began emptying out the Movers' attic, so I shapeshifted and started to follow him."

"That's why he kicked you," said Cleo. "He said there were mice everywhere."

"No," smiled Chillchase. "Just one very committed mouse."

"Sneer must have known the attic was where we'd go next," sighed Luke. "Mr Skipstone said we'd have to return the relics in the order we found them – so of course he was waiting for us. I never expected him to think ahead."

"Nor did I," said Resus. "But if we can't find Heru, the doorway will stay open for good."

"It won't," Chillchase assured them as he pulled himself to his feet. "It *can't*. Life is too dangerous for normals here in Scream Street."

"It's not exactly a picnic for them if G.H.O.U.L. catches them sniffing around, either," Cleo muttered.

"If the doorway remains open, it will only be a matter of time before G.H.O.U.L. discovers its existence," added the Tracker. "I've been able to hide it from them so far, but when they find out, they will almost certainly banish the three of you to the Underlands as punishment."

"Then we *have* to find Heru," Luke declared. "Wherever Sir Otto has sent him."

"He used an illegal spell to open a Hex Hatch for the Movers to pass through with Heru's sarcophagus," Zeal Chillchase said. "They returned empty-handed."

"Where did it lead?" Luke asked. "Where did they take him?

"I couldn't get close enough to see," Chillchase replied, "not without revealing myself – but I did manage to memorize the Hex Hatch's residual magic frequency."

Resus looked blank. "And for us non-brainiacs, that means…?"

Zeal Chillchase removed his mirrored sunglasses and stared soberly down at the trio. "It means I can open a Hex Hatch to exactly the same place," he said. "But I don't know where in the world it will take you."

Chapter Three
The Hex Hatch

The view through the rectangle in the air showed nothing but swirling violet light. Luke, Resus and Cleo gazed at it in trepidation.

The trio had helped the injured Zeal Chillchase to a quiet spot along one of the side streets, and when they were certain they wouldn't be disturbed by normals, the Tracker had stepped into a tree-lined garden and set about opening the Hex Hatch.

"OK..." said Resus eventually. "So, Sir Otto's hidden Heru *where*, exactly?"

"I can't tell," Zeal Chillchase admitted. "Usually Hex Hatches are opened with the knowledge of what's on the other side. Activating them by frequency alone doesn't allow light to pass through."

"But I thought Hex Hatches were like windows?" Luke protested. "You just open them and look through to the other side."

"It's not that simple," said Chillchase. "Think of it like finding the parts of a machine but not knowing what they'll build until you put them together correctly."

Suddenly the rectangle of swirling light twisted violently to the left, making everyone jump. The Tracker held his hands out in front of the light and mumbled a few words under his breath until it settled. "I'm afraid it's not very stable," he said apologetically.

"But it definitely leads somewhere safe?" asked Luke.

"It leads *somewhere*," the Tracker confirmed. "Whether or not that somewhere is safe is a different matter. Stepping through this Hex Hatch will require something of a leap of faith."

"Or a leap off a high cliff if we walk in the wrong direction," Resus remarked. "Or a stroll into a dragon's cave, or a walk towards the mouth of a ravenous—"

"Don't be daft," scolded Cleo. "The Movers who took Heru through came back alive, didn't they? And that was with only the sense of touch."

"They're immortal!" Resus cried. "They could have been chewed up and spat out by man-eating meatballs and they'd still have made it back alive!"

"The Movers returned entirely unharmed," Zeal assured them, clutching his hand to his painful ribs. "Now, enough delay. You must pass through."

"We don't need to go right this second, do we?" asked Cleo. "There must be enough time to get you some help, or at least get you to where you can lie down for a while."

"I agree," said Luke. "Even if Sir Otto has discovered we still have all five senses intact, he'll think we don't have a clue where Heru is. And you really don't look well; you're very pale."

"It'd be a good look if you were a vampire,"

Resus quipped. "But I'm not sure you should be sweating quite so much."

"There's no time!" Chillchase barked. "Besides," he continued more calmly, "I already have access to treatment..." He produced a half-empty bottle of wine from the pocket of his coat and pulled the cork out with his teeth.

"I'm not sure that's exactly what Dr Skully would recommend for broken ribs," commented Resus.

Chillchase up-ended the bottle and poured the contents onto the grass. Within seconds, the ground began to rumble and a rotten, scabby hand burst through the earth. A decomposed face appeared and began to suck up the wine.

"A Nineteen Forty-nine Chablis, drizzled over grass and crunchy insects. Bodacious cocktail, man!" When every drop had been consumed, the zombie clambered out of his tunnel and gazed blearily around him.

"Doug can help me to Everwell's Emporium after you've gone," said Chillchase. "Eefa has a superb spell for broken bones."

Cleo nodded. "He's right," she said. "Eefa made the pain completely vanish that time I broke my arm."

Doug blinked as if noticing the children for the first time. "Hey, little dudes!" he beamed through blackened teeth. "How are my three favourite adventurers doing?"

"Off on another one, I'm afraid," Luke replied. "Got a mummy to find and a relic to return."

Resus pulled the heart from his cape to show him.

Doug licked his lips. "Are you dudes going to eat that?"

Resus quickly slipped the heart away again. "It's not a snack, Doug!" he admonished.

The zombie sighed, then suddenly noticed the Hex Hatch. He stared, transfixed by the sight.

"*Whoa,* dude," he breathed. "That's, like, so *swirly*!"

"And it's as stable as I can make it," Zeal said, "but it won't stay like that for long. I shall return and reopen the Hatch once Eefa has treated my injuries, but you must go through it now."

Luke, Resus and Cleo shared a nervous glance, then stepped into the pulsating violet tunnel.

Luke hit the ground with a *thump*, biting his tongue and tasting blood. But there was something mixed in with the blood. Something gritty. Sand.

The journey through the Hex Hatch had been very strange. As soon as he had stepped through the window into the swirling purple tunnel, he had lost sight of Resus and Cleo and become aware of a collection of faces whooshing around his head. No, not faces – memories.

Moments from his life were twirling in the tunnel around him, like something out of a cartoon. There was the bully from his old school; Resus spraying his hair black on the day they'd first met; his mum's terrified expression as she underwent her first werewolf transfor—

Thump!

Resus landed beside Luke. The vampire lifted his head and tried to focus. "Doug was right," he gulped. "That was, like, so *swirly*!"

"Where are we?" asked Luke, sitting up and spitting the sand out of his mouth. He shielded his eyes against a blazing sun. The ground beneath him was hot to the touch.

"No idea," replied Resus, brushing sand off his own hands and looking around.

"I know where I am," squealed Cleo excitedly. "I'm home!"

The mummy was standing a few metres away and the boys climbed to their feet to join her. The sand stretched ahead for miles, and there in the middle distance stood several enormous pyramids.

Resus stared. "*That's* where you used to live?"

"Not in any of those," said Cleo. "My pyramid was in the Valley of the Queens, miles over that way – on the other side of the Nile." She pointed out across a seemingly endless desert.

"Valley of the Queens?" said Luke. "Is there something you're not telling us...?"

Cleo laughed. "Don't worry, there's nothing royal about me," she said. "I was a handmaiden,

nothing more. But I was buried in the same pyramid as my queen."

"Good," grinned Resus. "There's no way I'm going to start bowing down to you – even if you were a queen in some daft country."

"Hey!" Cleo scolded. "It's not 'some daft country'. It's Egypt! Come on." She set off in the direction of the pyramids.

"Egypt?" breathed Resus excitedly as he and Luke caught her up.

Cleo nodded. "I didn't realize G.H.O.U.L. still owned this part of it."

Resus was staring at the landscape around him, eyes wide. "I can't believe we're actually in Egypt…"

"Well, if all the sand and big, pointy buildings don't give it away, surely you should have noticed from the Sphinx."

Resus followed Cleo's gaze and his jaw dropped at the sight of a mammoth statue of a lion's body with a human head. "That's … HUGE!" he exclaimed.

"Certainly is," said Cleo proudly. "Took years to build, too. Although it looks like vandals have got to it recently – its nose is missing."

Luke fought the urge to smile. The Sphinx's nose had been missing in every picture he'd ever seen. "Who's buried in those?" he asked, gesturing towards the pyramids up ahead.

"I'm not sure about most of them," said Cleo. "But *that*," she added, pointing to the largest one, "is the final resting place of the great pharaoh … Heru!"

Chapter Four
The Pyramid

"Of course!" exclaimed Resus. "Sneer's sent Heru back home, just like Chillchase did with Count Negatov! It's obvious when you think about it."

"As obvious as pyramids telling you we're in Egypt?" smirked Cleo.

"Ha, ha."

"It's not all good news," Luke put in. "From what I remember, pyramids are sealed once the mummy's inside – and they're not designed to be reopened."

"Maybe," said Resus. "But we've got a local on our side: handmaiden Cleo Farr and her incredible skeleton key!" He bowed theatrically.

"Give over," Cleo said good-naturedly. "You were right – don't ever bow, it doesn't suit you."

The trio had now reached the foot of the pyramid, and Luke peered up at the colossal sloping sides, which disappeared into the glaring sun above. "I'm not sure any sort of key is going to help us get inside this," he said.

"But there has to be a way in," countered Resus. "The Movers must have carried Heru's sarcophagus inside." He turned to Cleo for inspiration.

"Don't look at me," she protested. "Each pyramid was built differently, with different entrances and exits. This one won't be the same as mine."

"Resus is right, though," said Luke. "The Movers had to get inside somehow, unless they dumped Heru in the desert and scuttled off home. Let's take a look around."

The trio began to explore the base of the pyramid, inspecting the bottom-most blocks of stone as they circled it. The sides were rough and weather-beaten, and chunks of rock had broken away, littering the ground.

The children ran their fingers along the fine gaps between the stone blocks, searching for anything that might indicate a hidden entrance – but there were no clues to be found. How the Movers had got inside remained a mystery.

An hour later they were back were they had started. "Nothing!" sighed Resus, wiping sweat from his brow. "And could this place *get* any hotter?"

Cleo glanced up at the cloudless sky. "It's actually quite mild today."

"Yeah, right," grumbled Resus, fanning his face with the edge of his cape. "And Samuel Skipstone's a champion mountain-climber!"

"That's an idea," said Luke.

"What?" spluttered Resus. "You want us to climb up there?"

"No," retorted Luke. "Mr Skipstone might know how to get inside." He pulled a gold-covered book out of his pocket. The title, *The*

G.H.O.U.L. Guide, was embossed along its spine.

"Ah ... Egypt," smiled the author, opening his eyes, which protruded from the front cover. "I haven't been here for many a year."

Samuel Skipstone had been one of Scream Street's founding fathers, and he had merged his spirit with the pages of one of his books in order to continue his research into the community. *The G.H.O.U.L. Guide* was his latest papery home.

"I'm afraid we won't be staying long if we can help it," said Luke. "But do you know how we can get in here?" He turned the book to face Heru's pyramid, and as he did so the glare of the sun reflecting off the cover shone in Resus's eyes.

The vampire quickly ducked under his cloak. "Watch out!" he shouted. "I might not shrivel up in the sun like other vampires, but that doesn't mean I want it beamed directly into my brain!"

"Sorry," said Luke, quickly angling the book away. As he moved it, the shaft of light raced up the side of the pyramid and settled over a bulge in the uneven rock. Suddenly there was a crunching sound and the block of stone in front of them began to slide inwards, creating a narrow entrance.

"A light-activated switch!" exclaimed Luke. He flipped the book over and grinned at the face on its cover. "Mr Skipstone – you're brilliant!"

The author looked up at him, confused. "I am?"

The tunnel was dark: much darker even than the Movers' attic. The stone doorway had remained open for only a few seconds, giving the children barely enough time to dart inside before the daylight was sealed off. Resus pulled out his flaming torch and led the way along a narrow passage.

"How do you reckon the Movers got in?" he asked. "They didn't have *The G.H.O.U.L. Guide* to bounce the sunlight off that sensor."

"Heru's sarcophagus is made from solid gold," Cleo reminded him. "That would work."

"The ground's starting to rise," Luke observed. "We're walking uphill. Do you reckon we're heading towards the centre of the pyramid?"

"Well, that's where the main tomb is in mine," said Cleo. "It would make sense for Heru's resting chamber to be in the same position."

The trio walked on in silence for a few more minutes, then Luke suddenly noticed a light up ahead. "I think we're almost there," he whispered.

They hurried faster along the tunnel and soon it began to widen, eventually opening out into a vast chamber. The children caught their breaths. Before them was more gold and treasure

than they could ever have imagined. And dozens more corridors led off from the chamber. They glimpsed other rooms beyond, all of them also piled high with gold.

The room was lit softly by some unseen glow from above, which sparkled off the heaps of gems. Resus slid the torch away and peered up at where the pyramid's four sloping walls narrowed and joined, shaking his head in amazement at the sheer scale of the building. "This place is massive," he breathed.

"There's an entire golden chariot over there!" exclaimed Luke.

"That will be so Heru can get around in the next life," Cleo explained, smiling at the boys' expressions of astonishment.

Resus grabbed a handful of gold coins from the ground by his feet. "Just one pocketful of this stuff could make us rich beyond our wildest dreams..."

"Don't you dare!" said Cleo.

"Think about it," Resus persisted. "We could buy Scream Street and get rid of Sneer once and for all!"

Cleo folded her arms. "Resus Negative, you

are not to take a single penny out of this pyramid. Do you hear me?"

"But..."

"No!" insisted the mummy. "This gold has been here for thousands of years."

"Then nobody needs it, do they?"

"Forget it, Resus," said Luke. "We're here to find Heru, give back his heart and go home. We're not touching the treasure."

"Especially as it's cursed," added a voice that came from the direction of Luke's pocket.

Luke pulled out *The G.H.O.U.L. Guide* once again. "Did you say *cursed*?" he asked the face of Samuel Skipstone.

"Indeed I did," replied the author, flipping the book open to a page showing an illustration of the very tomb in which they now stood. "Heru's treasure is guarded by all manner of powerful spells. Remove anything from the pyramid and you release the magic along with it. Who knows what the consequences of that might be?"

Resus pulled a face. "You don't believe any of that nonsense, do you?"

"There were many things I did not believe were possible before I was moved to Scream

Street," Skipstone replied mysteriously.

"There!" said Resus. "Mr Skipstone agrees with me. I think..."

"Cursed or not, this stuff doesn't belong to us," declared Luke. "Let's just find Heru and do what we're here to do."

"That could be tricky," said Cleo. "This place is massive, and we're looking for a golden sarcophagus hidden somewhere among vast piles of – guess what – gold!"

The G.H.O.U.L. Guide snapped shut and an expression of concern came over the golden face on the cover. "Miss Farr has a valid point," Samuel Skipstone said. "Please be careful not to set me down – you might never find me again!"

Luke tucked the book back into his pocket, then climbed onto the back of the golden chariot to get a better view of the chamber. The precious metal and jewels rose up in tall peaks on all sides.

"Heru must be in here somewhere," he contended. "The Movers won't have spent that long hiding him – there's no way Sneer expected us to get this far."

"It wouldn't have taken much," Cleo pointed out. "Shovel a pile of coins over his sarcophagus

and we could easily walk right past him without even knowing. It could take us years to search every inch of this place."

"I know what we need," said Resus. "Dave!"

Chapter Five

The Attack

"Dave?" said Luke. "Who's Dave?"

Resus reached into his cape and pulled out what looked like a large lump of writhing gristle. "This," he beamed, "is Dave!"

Cleo squealed and took a step backwards. "What *is* that thing?"

"It's a leech," Resus explained. "You're not the only one who likes animals, you know."

"That's not an animal!" cried Cleo. "It's a … *thing*! Where on earth did you get it?"

"I found him under a rock at the bottom of my garden," Resus explained.

Cleo didn't look convinced. "You found something *that* size under a rock?"

"Of course not," said Resus. "He was much smaller when I found him, but I've been feeding him up."

"On what?" demanded Luke.

Resus shrugged. "Leftovers from the zombies' bins, mainly," he answered. "That and other small animals. He's grown into a fine figure of a leech, don't you think?"

"It's grown into a *blob*!" exclaimed Cleo, repulsed.

"Maybe," Resus said defensively, "but a blob that might be able to help us find Heru."

"I don't get it," admitted Luke. "How can a fat, disgusting leech like that help us find Heru?"

"Do you mind?" snapped Resus. "You'll hurt his feelings." He stroked the creature's back and mumbled words of love into what he hoped was its ear.

"Sorry," said Luke, rolling his eyes. "What

I mean is, how can a magnificent specimen of leech-kind like Dave help us find Heru?"

"Simple," grinned Resus. He placed the leech on the floor and produced Heru's heart from his cloak. "Leeches like blood, right? Well, if we give Dave here a drop of Heru's blood, he'll get a taste for it and slither off to find some more."

Luke held up his hand. "Wait a minute," he said. "Are you trying to tell us that Dave is some kind of *sniffer* leech?"

"There's only one way to find out..." Resus held the heart out in front of Dave and squeezed it tightly. A few drops of thick, dark liquid forced themselves through a valve at the bottom and spattered to the ground. The leech slithered forward and sucked them noisily from the sand.

"I knew it wasn't completely dry!" exclaimed Resus, tucking the heart back into his cape.

"I think I'm going to be sick," groaned Cleo.

"Look!" cried Luke as the leech raised one end off the ground and appeared to sniff at the air. "I don't believe it. I think it's working!"

Slowly, Dave the leech began to wriggle towards a nearby pile of treasure. When it got there, it sucked a gold coin in through the gaping hole that was presumably its mouth and quickly expelled it from the other end, leaving the coin coated in a sticky, clear mucus. More coins and the occasional jewel fell to the same fate.

"And you wanted to take that stuff home with us," Luke said to Resus.

Before long the leech had vanished under the mound of treasure, although the trio could still hear the squelchy sucking noise as it progressed.

Cleo had her eyes screwed shut. "Tell me when it's over," she wailed.

"It will be pretty soon," Resus assured her. "If Dave has tunnelled into that pile, I'm willing to bet that's where the rest of Heru is."

"Then we'd better get him out before he ends up as leech food," suggested Luke. Grabbing a golden plate, he began to scoop coins from the pile. Resus found an urn and did the same.

Cleo gingerly plucked one coin at a time from the heap. "If I touch that thing – even accidentally – you'll pay," she growled at Resus.

A few minutes later, Luke stopped shovelling. "Look..." he hissed. Through the coins they could just about see a face made out of sapphires, rubies and diamonds. "That's Heru's face. It's the sarcophagus!"

The trio doubled their efforts until they had dragged the last of the treasure away from the coffin. Dave was slithering up and down on top of the lid, leaving glistening trails of goo in its wake.

Resus collected up the leech and tucked it back under his cloak. "Good boy," he crooned. "Go and find a treat: my Uncle Baz's spleen is in there somewhere."

Eep!

Cleo threw Resus a stern look. "*Eurgh!* Gross!"

Luke gripped the lid of the sarcophagus. "Ready?" he asked the others. Together, he, Resus and Cleo swung it open to reveal the mummified pharaoh. Heru's eyes flickered open.

"It's you three!" he cried joyfully. "Duke, Creases and Theo."

"Er … Luke, Resus and Cleo, actually," smiled Cleo. "But you were close…"

"I was, wasn't I?" beamed Heru. "Hooray for me! So – are we there yet?"

Luke wasn't quite sure how to reply. "Er … are we *where* yet?"

"That's just it," said Heru. "I don't know! Otto Sneer said the Movers were taking me on a little holiday – but he wouldn't say where."

"Don't get too excited," said Resus. "I think you've been here before..."

Heru sat up and gazed around him at the coins and jewels piled almost to the top of the cavern; the golden pillars studded with precious stones; chest after chest of glittering treasure. "Oh, goody," he squealed, clapping his hands. "I'm home. How lovely!"

Parp!

"It *would* be lovely if Resus's little pet would stop doing that," muttered Cleo, clamping her hand over her nose to block out the noxious gas.

"That wasn't Dave," insisted Resus. He winced as the stench reached his own nostrils. "In fact, if anything, that smells like..."

"CHARGE!"

Suddenly thousands of tiny, grey creatures stampeded into the cavern from every direction. They clambered over the mountains of coins, leapt out from behind golden pillars and jumped over chests of treasure. Occasionally one of them would let off a burst of gas from its behind, which would propel it forward a few metres.

"Oh no..." breathed Luke, his eyes wide with terror. "Goblins!"

The creatures were all over the trio in seconds, pushing them down and sitting on their arms, legs and shoulders. The children struggled to break free, but a couple of blasts of gas quickly subdued them.

Sitting up in his sarcophagus, Heru could not have been more delighted. "Entertainment, too," he enthused. "This is wonderful!"

"It's not wonderful," croaked Luke through a faceful of gas, "and nor is it entertain—"

He stopped. A small goblin had appeared in his line of vision and was now striding up his stomach. It stood to attention on his chest. "Squiffer," Luke growled.

"I might have known you'd be here!" yelled Cleo.

"You be silence!" shouted the goblin. "I be here to make special announce." The creature blasted a stinking fanfare from its bottom. "Please be bowing for glorious head of goblin family."

The other goblins chattered excitedly at the announcement. Resus tried unsuccessfully to shake a couple of them off his legs. "And how do you expect us to bow when you're holding us down?" he asked through gritted teeth.

Squiffer considered the problem for a second, then trumpeted a shorter fanfare. "Please be lying still for glorious head of goblin family."

A large goblin wearing a tin-foil cape and woollen baby booties strutted into view. He

paused at Luke's feet for a moment to survey his prisoners, then marched up to where Squiffer stood waiting.

"This be the Great Guff," proclaimed Squiffer. "He be lovely head of— *Aargh!*"

The Great Guff kicked Squiffer off Luke's chest. "They be know who the Great Guff is," he barked. "*Every* people be know who the Great Guff is!"

At this the rest of the goblins cheered and farted noisily. The Great Guff threw his arms in the air to accept the adulation, revealing gold bangles from wrist to shoulder.

"My jewellery as props, as well," squeaked Heru joyfully. "How can this performance get any better?"

"I tell you how," smirked the goblin leader. "Today be the day the Great Guff be get married!"

The goblins cheered again.

"Married?" exclaimed Cleo. "Who to?"

The Great Guff turned to indicate a small female goblin draped in so many gold chains that she could barely walk under the weight. "This be my soon wife," he crooned. "Princess Poot."

"Princess *Poot*?" spluttered Resus with a giggle.

The female goblin clambered across the mound of coins and bent down to press her face against the vampire's. "Yes," she blustered. "I be Princess Poot. This be princess bit…" She planted a kiss on Resus's lips. "…and this be poot!" She spun round and let off a burst of rancid fumes.

Eep!

"Yuk!" Resus closed his eyes and twisted his head from side to side, trying not to choke on the pungent gas. Goblins all over the tomb burst into laughter and added to the stench.

Heru looked as though he might faint with happiness. "A royal wedding!" he shrieked. "I must get dressed in my most regal finery…" He was just about to clamber out of his sarcophagus when a mob of goblins scurried over, each aiming a jewel-encrusted dagger at his chest.

"You be going nowhere," growled the Great Guff.

Chapter Six
The Lock

Heru sat back down again, his eyes wide as the points of the daggers pressed against his bandages. "I say," he cried. "This is hardly sporting! What's going on?"

"I was about to ask the same thing," said Luke.

The Great Guff picked up a diamond necklace from the mound of treasure at his large feet.

He paused to kiss Princess Poot on the cheek, then hung it around her neck. The weight finally became too much and the female goblin crashed face first into the treasure with a squeal.

"I be explain what be going on," declared the Great Guff loudly as his fiancée struggled to sit up. "Round smoke man give goblins many shiny 'longings if they be keep squishy pump from bandage wrap."

There was a brief silence while everyone ran through this sentence in their head a few times.

Resus was the first to speak. "Er … what?"

Luke sighed as the meaning of the goblin's words hit him. "He means that Sneer has promised the goblins all this treasure if they stop us from giving Heru back his heart."

"What?" exclaimed Heru. "But this isn't his treasure to give away! It's mine!"

"The heart is yours too," Cleo reminded him, "but that's Sneer for you."

"I'm one of Scream Street's founding fathers," protested Heru. "If some jumped-up landlord thinks he can treat me like this, he's got another think coming!"

"Round man be thinking you be saying that,"

said the Great Guff. "Goblins – be close bandage-wrap box!"

The goblins already surrounding Heru suddenly pushed the pharaoh flat on his back and slammed down the lid of the sarcophagus. The mummy hammered on the inside of the lid. "Help!" he yelled in a muffled voice.

The Great Guff gave a wicked smile and let out a rasp of gas. "Be take sparkle nose for goblin 'longings," he commanded. One of the goblin guards grasped hold of the diamond on the coffin lid that represented Heru's nose and twisted it until a loud *click!* echoed around the tomb.

"Oh no..." hissed Cleo, paling.

"What?" demanded Resus.

Before Cleo could reply, the Great Guff ordered the goblins to do the same with the remaining jewels.

"Be take sparkle eyes!"

Click! Click! The goblins turned two large sapphires in their casings and pulled them free.

"Be take sparkle mouth!"

Click! Click! Click! Three glistening rubies were plucked out by strong, leathery fingers.

The Great Guff grinned. "Now goblins be take away shiny stones."

Cleo struggled against her captors. "No, you can't!" she shouted. "If you take those jewels out of the pyramid, you'll bring the curse down upon us all!"

The goblin leader scuttled over to peer down at her. "No," he snarled, his breath almost as smelly as his trousers. "I be bring curse down on *you*!"

Princess Poot had finally managed to pull off the heavy necklaces and she now sat up, spitting out gold coins. "What I be miss?"

"You be miss nothing, my soon wife," beamed the Great Guff, taking her hand. "It all be start … now!" Screwing up his face, he let out the loudest rasp Luke, Resus or Cleo had ever heard. A cloud of green gas erupted from his behind.

At the signal, the goblins clutching the jewels from the sarcophagus raced away while the others whooped and pumped with delight. They jumped off the children's arms and legs and began to stuff as much treasure as they could into their pockets.

Resus sat up. "It's official," he said as the goblin leader and his fiancée ran out of the chamber,

hand in hand. "The Great Guff has finally gone insane."

"He's not insane," said Cleo, climbing to her feet and hurrying over to Heru's sarcophagus. "He's clever. Very, very clever."

"Clever?" asked Luke, joining her. "But he's let us go. Look – they're not interested in us any more." All around the tomb, goblins were giggling with delight as they gathered up fistfuls of treasure. "That doesn't seem very clever to me."

"He's made sure we can't return the heart, though," said Cleo unhappily.

"What?" cried Resus. "How?"

Cleo ran her fingers over the indentations in the golden face on the lid of the coffin. "Those jewels weren't just for show," she explained. "They were part of a locking mechanism put there to stop thieves breaking in and stealing the pharaoh's body."

Luke's face fell. "You mean..."

Cleo nodded. "Unless we can get those jewels back, Heru's sarcophagus will never be opened again."

Luke pressed his palm against the lid of the sarcophagus. "Just a bit of metal separating us from

the third founding father," he sighed. "Sneer's really got us this time."

"And Heru, too," Cleo reminded him. "He's stuck in there for all eternity now."

"This is ridiculous," moaned Resus. "OK, so we're missing a couple of jewels to activate a lock – but we're surrounded by treasure, remember. There must be other diamonds and rubies we can use."

"I've no idea if it'll work," said Cleo, "but it's worth a try."

"Right," said Luke. "We need one diamond, two sapphires and three rubies."

"Quite a shopping list," Resus commented.

The trio joined the goblins in rooting through the mounds of treasure. Two minutes later, Cleo had to choose a different pile to search as one of the foraging creatures trumped loudly upon discovering a chest filled with golden cutlery.

Luke pulled off his jumper and used it as a makeshift bag to collect a small pile of sparkling blue gems from beneath the golden chariot.

Resus was forced to wrestle a ruby out of the hands of a particularly fat goblin wearing a crown and twelve pairs of silver earrings.

Eventually the trio gathered around the sarcophagus again to combine their loot. "You're the expert with locks," said Luke, handing Resus a ruby.

The vampire took the precious stone and lowered it into one of three hollow dips that formed Heru's mouth. He twisted it left and right, but it wouldn't sit properly in the hole – or in either of the others.

The trio tried the gems one by one, but none of them matched well enough to slot in perfectly and turn the locks, despite Heru's constant encouragement from inside. "Come on! Even my dimmest slave could have unlocked this thing by now!"

Resus gripped a large diamond in his fist. "If we do get this open, I'm gonna shove this one right up his nose."

Luke almost got one of the eyes to twist into place out of sheer force, but he had to give up when the edges of the sapphire began to cut into his hand.

"It's no good," grunted Resus, hurling a ruby across the cavern in frustration. It knocked a goblin off the back of a hyena statue with a yelp. "They just don't fit."

Luke sighed. "I'm almost tempted to try to smash into the thing." He and Resus glanced at Cleo, expecting her to protest.

"Don't look at me," she declared. "I'm out of ideas too."

"Hmm. I might have something that could help…" Resus reached into his cape and produced a spiked metal ball that was connected to a wooden handle by a thick chain. "The mace," he beamed. "A little souvenir from Count Negatov's castle."

Luke took the weapon from him. "Heru – it's Luke," he called out. "We're going to try to break you out. You might feel a little bump…"

"A *little* bump?" said Cleo.

"OK, then," called Luke, "a *big* bump!"

"Something between the end of the world and a planet dropping on your head," added Resus.

Luke readied himself. "One … two … three!" Swinging the mace high into the air, he smashed the ball against the lid of the sarcophagus. There was a loud *clang!* that sounded like a gong exploding, then the ball ricocheted backwards, pulling Luke off his feet and dragging the spiked ball from his grip.

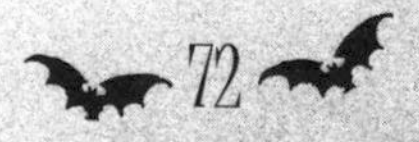

Resus and Cleo hurried over to help him up.

"Forget about me," insisted Luke. "Have we broken the lock?"

Cleo dropped to her knees and examined the image of Heru. "Not even a scratch," she sighed.

"Maybe not," yelled a muffled voice from inside the coffin, "but you've just given me a headache that'll last the next ten years. DO NOT do that again!"

Luke sat down heavily on the sarcophagus. "It's no good," he said. "We need to find the original jewels or this thing will stay shut for good."

"We've got more chance of stopping the Great Guff and Princess Poot from swapping gas," scoffed Resus.

"Swapping what?" asked Luke.

"Swapping gas," explained Resus. "It's how goblins get married. They don't exchange wedding vows, they…" He pulled a face as an unpleasant image flashed across his mind. "They squeeze into the smallest space they can find, then spend an entire twenty-four hours blasting gas at each other."

Cleo shuddered. "Gross!"

"Tell me about it."

Suddenly the trio heard a distant crash and the tomb began to shake from side to side, toppling mounds of treasure and burying a few unlucky goblins in the process.

"What was that?" demanded Resus.

"I don't know," admitted Luke as a second bang shook the cavern. A nearby pile of coins tumbled to the floor in a small avalanche of gold.

"I think I do," gulped Cleo. The boys looked at her. "The goblins must have started leaving the pyramid with Heru's treasure…"

Another thunderous crash shook the room.

Luke paled. "They've unleashed the curse!"

Chapter Seven
The Water

Luke held up the flaming torch as he, Resus and Cleo raced along a tunnel lined with silver statues of mermaids. To begin with the trio had tried to escape the way they had come, but the shockwaves that were rocking the pyramid had sent a pair of golden dog sculptures crashing down into the passageway, blocking their route.

"I don't feel good about leaving Heru behind!" yelled Cleo, leaping over a toppled mermaid.

"You'd feel worse if you stayed and the entire

tomb came down on top of you," Resus pointed out.

"Heru's sarcophagus is strong," Luke reassured her. "Short of the entire pyramid coming crashing down, it'll protect him from anything."

"And if the entire pyramid *does* come crashing down…?"

Luke shrugged. "Then giving back the heart will be the least of our worries."

Another boom rocked the ground beneath their feet and they were forced to press themselves against the walls of the tunnel to stay upright. Dozens more solid silver mermaids fell to the ground around them.

"'Subtle' wasn't exactly Heru's choice of decoration, was it?" quipped Resus. "I mean, why have one mermaid statue when you can ha— *Whoa!*"

Suddenly he disappeared from sight.

Luke just caught a glimpse of the vampire's cape disappearing over a ledge in the darkness ahead. He lunged forward and grabbed the end of it, managing to stop Resus's fall.

"Where did the floor go?" Resus called up, his voice echoing loudly around the tunnel.

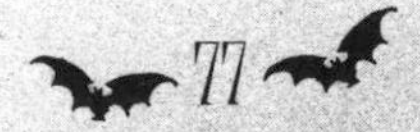

Gritting his teeth, Luke rested the flaming torch against the wall and began to pull on Resus's cape. Cleo hurried over to help, and between the two of them they were able to drag their friend back from the edge.

Resus collapsed onto the solid ground of the tunnel, trying to catch his breath.

"I thought that fall was going to kill you!" exclaimed Cleo.

"It's not the fall I was worried about," gasped Resus. "It was the sudden stop when I reached the bottom!"

Luke picked up the torch again and crawled back to the spot where the ground fell away. Below was a long drop down to another cavern. This one was smaller than Heru's tomb but lined with white marble and lit by fiery sconces attached to the walls. And there, filling almost the entire floor of the cavern, was… No – it couldn't be…

"Is that a *swimming pool*?" asked Luke incredulously.

Cleo and Resus joined him to gaze over the edge. "Yep," the mummy agreed. "That's a swimming pool!"

"Now I *know* that you mummies have more money than sense," remarked Resus. "Why would someone who is – to all intents and purposes – dead need one of those in their final resting place?"

The swimming pool was rectangular, and on each side was a row of more mermaid statues. The water in the pool was crystal clear.

As his eyes grew used to the dim light, Luke spotted something else. All around the pool were goblins, skipping and dancing at the water's edge. "They seem to be excited about something," he said.

"Probably the fact that they've taken away the steps they used to get down there," suggested Cleo, pointing to a pair of long, golden ladders lying at the side of the pool.

"Possibly," said Luke, "although they must know we'll try to get down another way."

"Wait... There!" hissed Resus, pointing. "There's something at the bottom of the pool ... something glinting." He pulled a pair of binoculars from his cloak and trained them on the water below. "Rubies!" he exclaimed, handing them to Luke. "I bet they're the three rubies the goblins took from Heru's sarcophagus."

Luke held the binoculars up to his eyes and adjusted the focus. Resus was right: there, on the bottom of the pool, lay three large rubies.

"How do we know they're the same ones?"

"We can't be certain," Resus admitted, "but it's a bit of a coincidence, isn't it? Exactly three rubies..."

"But why throw them into the pool?" asked Cleo. "That's a terrible hiding place."

"Goblins are notoriously scared of water," replied Resus. "It turns their gas into goo and causes them to swell up until they explode."

"Eurgh!" said Cleo. "I don't like the sound of that."

"Neither do I," agreed Resus, "and if the goblins think we're as scared as they are, it'll explain why they thought the pool was a safe place for the rubies."

"Well, I'm not scared of water," said Luke, "so our luck could finally be changing. The problem is – how do we get down without ladders?"

"I've got some rope in here somewhere," said Resus, plunging his hand into his cape.

"We don't need rope," scoffed Cleo. "I'm not scared of water either!" And, without another word, she leapt off the ledge and down into the cavern below.

Luke watched, open-mouthed, as she broke the surface of the water. "What did she do that for?"

"Because she's got about as much brain as a vegetarian zombie!" replied Resus. "Still, at least she'll be able to get the rubies for us."

"That's not the bit I'm worried about," said Luke. "Don't forget, once she's got the rubies, she'll have to climb out of the pool..."

With horror, Resus realized what Luke

meant. "And she'll be surrounded by all those goblins … alone!"

"Exactly," said Luke, jumping to his feet. He pulled *The G.H.O.U.L. Guide* from his pocket and handed it to Resus. "Look after Mr Skipstone for me."

"Why?" demanded Resus. "Wait a minute. You're not going to…"

Luke looked down at the surface of the swimming pool far below. "Yep, that's exactly what I'm going to do." Then he lifted his arms above his head, brought them together and dived off the ledge.

The air whipped around Luke's ears as he plunged down towards the water. He could see the goblins looking up and pointing at him as he dropped closer and closer. There was Cleo, her bandages soaked, kicking down towards the rubies resting on the marbled bottom…

Splash! The water enveloped Luke completely. It was far colder than he could possibly have imagined, and for a moment it felt as though all the wind had been knocked out of his chest.

He kicked his legs, twisted round and swam for the surface. He could hear the goblins' muffled

screeches and catcalls suddenly growing loud and echoing around the cavern as he burst up out of the water. He gulped down lungfuls of air as Cleo surfaced beside him.

"Cold, isn't it?" she grinned, her teeth chattering.

"What do you think you're doing?" Luke reprimanded. "You shouldn't have jumped from so far up."

"Oh, stop complaining," retorted Cleo. "Look – I've managed to get one of the rubies..." She held the sparkling red gem up out of the water. At the sight of it, the goblins around the pool went crazy.

"Hide it, quick!" Luke hissed. "You don't know what they'll do to get it back."

"Relax," Cleo insisted as she tucked the ruby into her bandages. The goblins began to run around the sides of the pool, pushing the mermaid statues into the water. "They're too scared to come in the water, and wrecking the place won't get them anywhere."

Luke felt something brush past his leg and his breath caught in his chest. "Don't speak too soon," he gulped.

Suddenly a shoal of silver mermaids rose up out of the water in front of them, now very much alive. Their shimmering hair lay slick against their scalps and their eyes shone bright green.

More and more of them surfaced until they completely encircled the children. They opened their beautiful mouths and hissed angrily, revealing sharp, pointed teeth.

Luke shivered. "I think we might be in a bit of trouble."

Chapter Eight
The Laughter

Resus let go of the rope and dropped the last few metres to the ground. He sped along the edge of the pool, dodging goblins as he ran, and opened *The G.H.O.U.L. Guide* to a page featuring one of the terrifying mermaids.

"Luke!" he yelled, skidding to a halt on the wet marble and turning the book round to show his friend. "Stay away from the statues – the goblins didn't think we were scared of water, they planned this. It's a trap!"

Luke and Cleo were now treading water in the middle of the swimming pool surrounded by hissing, snarling monsters. "Tell me something I don't know…" Luke called back.

"OK," shouted Resus. "They're not real mermaids – they're scaremaids!"

"Scaremaids?" demanded Cleo.

Resus nodded and read aloud from the pages of the golden book. *"Scaremaids are a cross between standard mermaids and sharks, bred originally to protect the kingdom of Atlantis. The creatures vanished without trace from the oceans around a thousand years ago."*

"I think we've found out where they all went," puffed Luke.

Samuel Skipstone watched, concerned, from the cover of the book. "The magic in Heru's curse must have reanimated them when they hit the water," he said. "You need to get out of the pool … now!"

"We're trying!" cried Luke. "We just have to

get past..." His words were lost in the churning of water as the scaremaids came in for the attack.

Luke felt sharp, pointed teeth bite at him and long, slender hands begin to pull him down. He just managed to take a deep breath before he was dragged beneath the surface. Through the clear water he could see Cleo's legs kicking furiously beside him and the scaremaids circling, teeth bared and eyes burning with emerald light.

Resus grabbed the end of one of the ladders lying at the pool side and tried to haul it towards the water, but it was far too heavy for him to move by himself.

In the water, the scaremaids continued to nip and bite at Luke's arms and legs. Twisting round, he found himself face to face with Cleo, who looked at him in terror as six of the scaremaids tore at her bandages with their fangs. Their silver tails thrashed wildly as they attacked their helpless prey.

Bubbles of air burst from Luke's mouth in a silent scream and his lungs began to burn. He had to get to the surface, had to breathe... Was this how he would die? Torn to pieces underwater? Anger flooded Luke's mind at the thought

of never returning home to Scream Street, never seeing his parents again.

He felt blackness wash over him and a jolt of pain shoot down his spine. For a split second he thought one of the scaremaids had bitten him on the back, but as his face stretched out to form a long snout and thick, brown fur emerged from the pores of his skin, he realized he was transforming into his werewolf.

Suddenly Luke no longer felt the urgency to reach the surface. His lungs – like the rest of his body – had changed shape, becoming more powerful and efficient in the process.

Now a fully formed wolf, Luke pumped his hind legs and shot through the water towards Cleo. The mummy's eyes were closed and the last human thought in Luke's mind was that he might already be too late. Gripping the nearest scaremaid in his powerful jaws, he slung the creature out of the pool. It landed on the narrow marble walkway and instantly became nothing more than a harmless silver statue again.

Luke's werewolf lashed out with its paws, dragging scaremaid after scaremaid away from Cleo. One of them had its teeth locked around

the mummy's throat, and the werewolf bit down hard on its thick tail, drawing opaque plumes of silver blood. Wrapping his front legs around Cleo, Luke swam up through the rapidly clouding water into the cool air above. When they broke the surface, Cleo opened her eyes and breathed long and hard.

"Behind you!" Resus's voice echoed off the marble walls and Luke's wolf turned to see half a

dozen more scaremaids zipping through the water towards them. He kicked his legs but couldn't move quickly enough and the scaremaids leapt from the water, as graceful as dolphins, before crashing down on top of him and dragging him beneath the surface once more.

One of them wrapped her arms around Luke's neck and the wolf's furry tail shot up involuntarily and brushed against her silver fins.

That's when the laughter started.

Beautiful, sing-song giggles suddenly filled the pool, borne upwards in tiny silver bubbles. Cleo's head whipped round to try to see where the sound was coming from, and she quickly realized that the scaremaid clinging to Luke's back was laughing uncontrollably.

At the pool side, Resus flipped frantically through the pages of *The G.H.O.U.L. Guide*. "That's it!" he exclaimed when he found the relevant entry. "Scaremaids respond to being tickled!"

"Tickled?" cried Cleo. "Have you been at Heru's wine cellar or something?"

"Master Negative is correct," agreed Samuel Skipstone. "Laughter overpowers the scaremaids,

and tickling them appears to be the most effective way to achieve this. It was for this reason that they were eventually relieved of their posts as guardians of Atlantis."

Resus pulled a feather duster from his cloak and tossed it down to Cleo. "Off you go, then," he grinned. "Get tickling!"

Cleo dived beneath the surface once again and slid the duster under the armpit of the nearest scaremaid. The creature's expression of fury turned to one of mirth as she too began to giggle. The mummy gripped her by the tail and found she was able to drag her over to the edge of the pool – tickling all the while – where Resus pulled her from the water and watched her solidify into a grinning silver figurine.

Cleo swam back into the middle of the pool, working the feather duster like a fencing foil, jabbing it here and there until the scaremaids around Luke were all rendered helpless with laughter. The water sparkled with millions of tiny, happy bubbles. It was like swimming in silver champagne.

Luke took Cleo's lead, tickling with his bushy tail and whiskers until eventually all the scare-

maids lay on the slick marble floor, transformed back to solid silver with their faces split into wide grins. The werewolf slumped at Resus's feet, shivering as its muscles reshaped and it became human once more. Cleo took the opportunity to dive back into the murky water and retrieve the final two rubies.

"We're halfway there," she grinned as she climbed out of the swimming pool, accidentally splashing a few drops of water over Resus's pristine shoes as she did so.

"Oi," snapped the

vampire. "Don't get me wet."

"I'll throw you in there if you start complaining," grunted Luke, climbing to his feet. "Cleo and I are soaked!"

"Yes, but I found out how you could defeat the scaremaids," countered Resus.

"*You* found that out, did you?" remarked Samuel Skipstone with a grin. "And here I was thinking that the answer lay in my years of painstaking research..."

Resus felt his cheeks redden. "Er ... yes, but I turned the pages!"

Luke patted his friend on the back and laughed. "And a brilliant job you did of it, too," he beamed. "Now we just have to get past these—"

He stopped and looked around him, suddenly realizing they were now alone. "Hang on – where did all the goblins go?"

There was a rumbling sound and the cavern began to shake.

Cleo shrugged. "Maybe the scaremaids frightened them off?"

"I wouldn't have thought so," said Luke. "They only came to life when they hit the water

– and the goblins were intent on staying as dry as Resus."

"Do you mind?"

The rumbling grew louder.

"No," continued Luke, "something else scared them away. I just can't think—"

He stopped again as the wall behind them exploded in a shower of marble. Chunks of stone rained down onto the floor and into the pool.

Then a worm the size of a train burst through and swallowed the trio whole.

Chaper Nine
The Slime

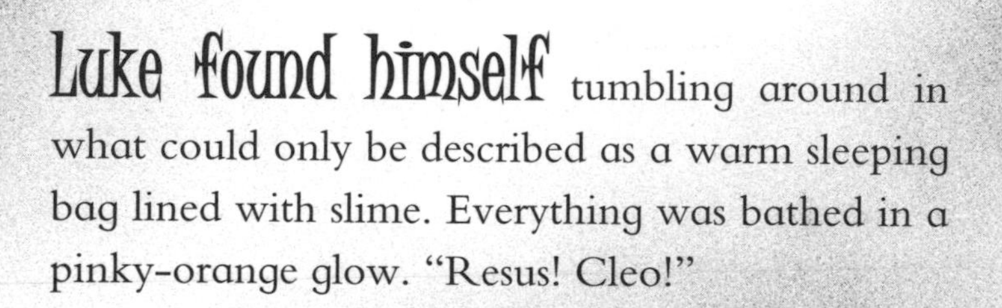

Luke found himself tumbling around in what could only be described as a warm sleeping bag lined with slime. Everything was bathed in a pinky-orange glow. "Resus! Cleo!"

"I'm here," replied Resus, slithering through the gloopy tunnel behind him. "Are you OK?"

"I think so..." Luke touched the wall and it undulated back and forth beneath his fingertips. "Please tell me we're not where I think we are..."

Resus nodded, droplets of slime bouncing off his nose. "'Fraid so. We've been eaten by some kind of giant worm." There was a loud crash that sent the boys sprawling. "And I'm pretty sure that was it smashing through another wall."

"That must have been what was rocking the pyramid," said Luke, kneeling upright. "I'm starting to believe in that curse after all." He looked around. "Where's Cleo?" he asked, suddenly realizing that she wasn't with them.

"Here," came a muffled voice. "And you won't believe who's with me..."

The boys crawled deeper into the worm, trying to keep their balance as it rocked and twisted from side to side. Before long they spotted something shining in the pink glow and Luke was amazed to see Cleo sitting on top of Heru's sarcophagus. "What's *that* doing here?"

"I think the worm must have taken a short-cut through the tomb," replied Cleo. "And look

– the sarcophagus wasn't the only thing it picked up along the way…" She lifted a fold of sticky worm intestine to reveal a small collection of treasure, the entire golden chariot and a dozen or so statues.

"It looks like we got out of Heru's tomb just in time," said Resus.

"Yeah," Luke retorted sarcastically. "I'd hate to have missed fighting the mental mermaids before the worm swallowed us."

Another crash flipped the trio upside down.

Cleo began to wipe the slime off her bandages. "Of all the things I've been through since I met you, Luke Watson, this counts as the worst!"

"Speaking of 'going through' things…" began Resus.

Cleo scowled. "I don't like the sound of this."

"I'm pretty sure I saw teeth as I was gulped down," continued the vampire. "Which means we probably can't get back out *that* end."

Cleo pressed her hands over her ears. "I'm not listening…"

"The other end might be the only way out, Cleo," said Luke.

Resus pulled a sword from his cape and pointed the blade towards the slimy wall. "I suppose we could always just cut our way free."

Cleo snatched the sword away from him. "No!" she snapped. "You can't. OK, so this thing might have tried to eat us, but it's a living animal."

"It didn't *try* to eat us, Cleo!" exclaimed Resus. "It *did* eat us!"

"I don't care," retorted the mummy. "It's only doing what's natural, and you're not going to hurt it – even if that does mean we have to take the … take the…" Her words trailed off and she looked around her, confused.

There was another violent crash and the worm twisted sharply to the left.

Luke crawled through a puddle of gloop to reach her. "What's wrong?"

"I… I don't know…" replied Cleo groggily. "Just feel … odd…"

Suddenly the worm gulped and undulated, and a screeching goblin swept down the creature's throat, landing at Resus's feet.

"Squiffer!" exclaimed Cleo.

"Oh, great," groaned the vampire. "Just what

we need. Another … er … another … what are these horrible things called, again?"

The goblin sat upright. "Squiffer be not horrible," he protested. "Squiffer be…" Then he collapsed, out cold.

"He's gone asleep," slurred Resus. "Actually … not bad idea…" He lay down and closed his eyes.

Luke shook him. "Resus! No! Wake up!"

The vampire opened his eyes. "Wassa marra?"

"Something's wrong," said Luke, trying to prop his friend up against the sarcophagus.

"Ooh, look," hissed Resus, pointing at the goblin. "He'ssss got the smaph … phass …

sapphham…" He took a deep breath. "He'ss got the blue onesssss…" Then his eyes closed again and his head sagged forward.

Luke turned to see that Resus was correct. The unconscious Squiffer had a large sapphire clamped in each hand. Luke pulled them free and stuffed them into his pocket.

Behind him, Cleo slumped over, moaning softly.

Luke reached into his other pocket for *The G.H.O.U.L. Guide*, panicking when he couldn't find it. Then he remembered handing it to Resus before he dived into the … dived into the … what was it he'd dived into?

It felt like his mind was obscured by a dense fog and every thought was coated in thick treacle. He had to get everyone out of here.

Luke's vision began to blur, and it took three attempts for him to slip his hand under Resus's cape and retrieve the golden book. "Wasss goin' on, Misser Skipsssone? Wasss happnin' to usss…?"

The author frowned. "You're inside a chloroworm, Luke – almost certainly brought into existence by Heru's curse. The chloroworm swallows its food whole, then uses an anaesthetic in its stomach to render victims unconscious so it can digest them at its leisure."

"Digessss atisss leisssurrreee?" slurred Luke.

"Luke, you have to listen to me!" shouted Skipstone. With a supreme effort, Luke managed to get his eyes to focus on the friendly face. "You have to get yourself, Resus and Cleo out of here – now! If you pass out, you'll never wake up again."

Luke nodded and climbed numbly to his feet, tucking the book away. His friends were snoring away happily in pools of slime: Resus was leaning against Heru's sarcophagus and Cleo's head was resting against the wheel of the golden chariot.

The chariot – that was it! Maybe he could use the chariot to drag everyone out of the worm before it was too late.

Struggling to retain consciousness, Luke pulled Cleo up and onto the platform of the chariot, then crawled back along the chloroworm's intestines and did the same with Resus.

Then his eyes rested on the sleeping figure of Squiffer, and briefly he wondered if he should leave him to be digested. But – unconscious or not – he could almost hear Cleo nagging in his

ear, and he tossed the goblin onto the platform beside his friends. Squiffer gave a gentle *eep*, filling the air with stinking green fumes.

Luke grabbed a length of gold chain that was attached to the back of the chariot and tied it around Heru's sarcophagus in what he hoped was a workable knot. His mind was beginning to shut down and he was finding it difficult to see or hear.

Now he just had to attach the reins to the inside of the ... the inside of the... No, that could wait until he'd had a bit of a rest. It wouldn't matter too much if he had a quick nap – he could carry on rescuing his friends after that...

As Luke lay his head down beside Resus and Cleo, faces floated through his mind, the same faces he had seen when he'd passed through the Hex Hatch that morning. He saw the bully from his old school taunting him, Resus spraying dye over his hair on the day they'd first met, and his mum laughing as she struggled to beat his score on his favourite computer game...

The thought of his mum jerked Luke back to reality and he pulled himself to his feet. His mum was back in Scream Street and she needed his help to cope with her werewolf transformations. He had to get out of here – and home.

The chariot had two leather reins, each one ending in a sharp, metal spike. Luke plunged the first one into the soft, jelly-like stomach of the chloroworm. The creature screeched and twisted angrily, but Luke managed to keep his balance as he embedded the second hook. Now he just had to find a way to get the chariot moving.

Squiffer murmured softly in his sleep and turned over, more noxious fumes pumping from his behind as he did so. Good thing I don't need a flaming torch in here, thought Luke groggily, or I'd be…

The torch! That was it! It would be dangerous, but perhaps the only way out. Lifting Resus's cape, Luke rummaged inside until he found the burning length of wood. Then he held the flame over the goblin's behind and closed his eyes.

Chapter Ten
The Wedding

The golden chariot shot out of the chloroworm's back end in an explosion of goblin gas, dragging Heru's sarcophagus behind it. The reins pulled taut just as the wheels hit the ground and began to spin for the first time in thousands of years.

Cautiously, Luke opened his eyes – just in time to see the worm charge angrily for the nearest wall. Giant blocks of thick, heavy stone rose up as far as the eye could see. There was no way the worm, or the chariot, would survive the impact.

Luke barely had time to brace himself for the collision when instead the worm plunged down into the sand and began to dig with its jaws. Without losing speed, the creature excavated a makeshift tunnel and plunged into it, chariot and all.

Foul, slimy sand erupted from the creature's back end and Luke ducked behind the chariot's front shield to avoid being swept away. Then, in what seemed like no time at all, the chloroworm changed direction and climbed back up towards the surface.

Resus woke just as the worm burst through the hot sand and into the glaring sunshine. "Watson!" he yelled. "What have you *done*?"

"I've got us out!" Luke shouted back as the worm began to drag the chariot across the desert. "And not a moment too soon. We were being digested in there!"

Cleo opened her eyes and found Squiffer

curled up on her lap. She squealed and pushed him away.

The goblin bounced off the platform of the chariot and onto the sand, where he sat up groggily, clutching his head. "What be Squiffer drinking last night?"

The mummy clambered to her feet and joined Luke and Resus at the front of the chariot, holding on for dear life. "What's going on?" she cried.

"Luke's finding new and unusual ways to kill us!" Resus bellowed back.

"Excuse me!" shouted Luke, keeping a tight grip on the reins. "Thanks to me, we've got the three rubies *and* the two sapphires for the top of Heru's sarcophagus. We just need the diamond and we can open it again."

"But we don't know where the diamond is," countered Cleo.

A glint caught Luke's eye and he squinted against the glare of the sun to get a better look. "I think we might have just found it…" he said.

Cleo and Resus followed Luke's gaze. Some distance away, hundreds of goblins were arranged in rows on the sand. The Great Guff and Princess Poot seemed to be proceeding between the rows,

and the sparkle was coming from a ring on the bride's finger.

"The royal wedding!" exclaimed Cleo.

Luke nodded, pulling slightly on the right-hand rein to adjust the worm's course. "And I bet the diamond was the gemstone the goblins took out of the pyramid, triggering the treasure's curse."

"I *told* you it was all true," snapped Cleo.

"There'll be time for you to gloat later," retorted Resus as the chariot hit a sand dune and lurched violently to the left. "At least, I hope there will!"

"But how do we get the diamond back?" asked Cleo.

"Resus can take the reins and you can snatch the diamond as we go past," instructed Luke. "I'm going to slot the other gems into their holes."

Cleo looked back at the golden sarcophagus swinging wildly from side to side behind the chariot. "While we're still moving?"

"If we stop, the goblins will be all over us," said Luke as he thrust the reins into Resus's hands and hurried to the back of the platform. He gritted his teeth and leapt across the gap to the sarcophagus, landing on top of it with a *thump!*

"Who's there?" demanded Heru from inside. "What's going on?"

Luke glanced up towards Resus, who was now steering the chloroworm towards the goblin wedding. "You wouldn't believe me if I told you," he shouted back. "Just hang on, and we'll have you out of there."

Luke was now crouching on top of the sarcophagus, grasping the chain with one hand to avoid falling off. He steadied himself and took the first ruby out of his pocket. He slotted it carefully into the correct recess on the lid and twisted. The lock gave a *click*. "It's working!" he yelled, taking out the next ruby. "Get that diamond!"

The Great Guff didn't look up until the worm was almost upon him. Resus shook the reins and urged the creature onwards. Its teeth gnashed hungrily as it became aware of the goblins in its path.

Cleo suddenly grabbed one of the leather straps and pulled hard, causing the worm to swerve. "None of them gets eaten!" she ordered.

"You're not making this easy," called Resus, swinging the worm back towards the wedding

and fighting to steer its snapping jaws away from the terrified guests.

"What be going on?" the Great Guff screamed angrily as the worm shot past.

Cleo reached down out of the chariot and plucked the massive diamond from the ring on Princess Poot's finger. "This isn't yours!" she yelled.

The family of goblins leapt to their feet in rage, only to be knocked off them again as Resus circled back round and Heru's sarcophagus ploughed through them. Luke, now lying flat on top of it to keep his balance, twisted the final sapphire eye into place.

"That's it!" he shouted. "Now I just need the diamond!"

Cleo carefully made her way to the back of the chariot, unaware that the goblins were now angrily giving chase. As she stretched out her hand towards Luke, she suddenly spotted something on the sarcophagus lid behind him. Two somethings…

"Luke!" she called. "Behind you!"

Luke twisted round to see the Great Guff and Princess Poot clinging onto the golden casket,

their big leathery ears flapping in the wind. "You be give me shiny stone!" roared the goblin leader, crawling towards him.

Luke turned back to Cleo and urged her on. "Quick!" he shouted. The mummy gripped the back of the platform with one hand and stretched out the other. Luke's fingertips brushed the diamond … he almost had it…

Princess Poot raced up Luke's back and snatched the gem from Cleo's fingers. "If I can't be have shiny stone, no one be have it!" And she gave a loud *eep!* and held the diamond into the flow of gas, where it melted away.

"Goblin guff!" Cleo cried. "The only substance in the world that can destroy diamonds!"

Luke stared in horror, but he didn't have time to dwell on it.

"Pyramid alert!" bellowed Resus. Luke and Cleo turned their attention back to the chariot to discover that they were almost back at Heru's pyramid. In fact, they were charging towards it at breakneck speed…

"Go up!" hollered Luke.

Obediently, Resus pulled back hard on the reins, lifting the chloroworm's head just as it was

about to dig another tunnel. The creature gave a screech and began to charge up the slope towards the peak, still dragging the chariot and sarcophagus behind.

As the worm reached the top of the pyramid, Resus pulled out his sword and sliced through the reins. Free at last, the chloroworm let loose another terrifying cry, then began to slither down the other side. When it reached the ground, it opened its gargantuan jaws and dug into the sand. Within seconds it had disappeared from view, the hole collapsing in behind it. Both Luke and the sarcophagus were flung onto the back of the chariot with a *crash!*

Then silence filled the desert. And the golden chariot sat balanced on the tip of the pyramid, rocking gently back and forth in the warm desert breeze.

Chapter Eleven
The Key

Luke took a deep breath. "No one move," he hissed. The wheels of the golden chariot spun to a stop.

"We can't stay up here," said Cleo.

"We can't risk rolling down the side of the pyramid, either," whispered Luke. "This thing hasn't got any brakes: we'd slam straight into the ground."

"So, what do we do?" asked Cleo, gripping onto the chariot as a gust of wind threatened to push it over the edge.

Resus risked a cautious glimpse over the side. "Whatever we do, we need to do it quickly..."

The Great Guff and Princess Poot were already leading the pack of angry goblins up the slope of the pyramid towards them.

"Goblins be take back shiny stones," growled the Great Guff. "I be toss pesky kids off top of pointy house."

"Look!" cried Cleo, pointing at something on the other side of the pyramid. A swirly, purple window had appeared a few metres above the ground. "It's a Hex Hatch!" she exclaimed. "Mr Chillchase has opened another Hex Hatch for us!"

"Maybe we could climb out and slide down towards it," Resus said thoughtfully.

"*Slide?* On what?"

Resus shrugged. "Our bottoms? OK, so it'll hurt, but at least we'll get down alive. Well, more alive than if the goblins get to us!"

Luke looked wistfully down at the sapphires and rubies fixed in position on the image of the

pharaoh's face, and then at the space where the diamond should be. "It means we'll have to go home without returning Heru's heart," he sighed. "There's no way we can get this open now."

Cleo pulled the skeleton key from her bandages. "What about this?"

Resus and Luke looked at one another. Could the key work in the final section of the lock? There was only one way to find out…

Taking the skeleton key from Cleo, Luke leant over the back of the chariot and stretched out his hand towards the far end of the sarcophagus. The carriage tipped slightly but stayed balanced as he pressed the finger bones into the dip above the image of Heru's nostrils.

"Quickly," urged Resus. "The goblins are getting close." The Great Guff and his army were now using blasts of goblin gas to aid their ascent.

Slowly, the key began to expand until it exactly fitted the diamond-shaped hole. With a trembling hand, Luke turned the key in the lock.

Click!

The lid of the sarcophagus swung open and Heru climbed out. "That's more like it!" he cried,

leaping onto the chariot and causing it to wobble violently. He appeared not to have noticed their predicament. "Now, are you any good at sewing?"

"Sewing?" asked Cleo. "What on earth for?"

"I shall need a new outfit for the royal wedding, of course," beamed the pharaoh. His face suddenly fell. "Oh no – I haven't missed it, have I?"

"No," growled a voice behind them. "You be just in time." The Great Guff and Princess Poot, at the head of the goblin mob, clambered over the sarcophagus and onto the platform of the chariot, where their weight finally upset the balance.

With a shriek of metal against stone, the chariot rocked violently for a few moments before tipping backwards and beginning to roll down the side of the pyramid, slowly at first, dragging the sarcophagus with it.

Hundreds of goblins, tired and aching from their climb, looked up with wide eyes as the golden carriage picked up speed, plunging towards them. Those lucky enough to leap out of the way lost their grip on the stone and found themselves tumbling head over heels back down towards the ground.

Squiffer, at the back of the pack, gave a small *eep!* of gas as the chariot headed straight for him. "This be not my day," he squeaked as he disappeared beneath the vast wheels.

Luke, Resus, Cleo and Heru clung on to each other as the carriage continued to pick up speed.

"What be going on?" screamed Princess Poot. "I only want be married!"

"My pleasure," grinned Resus, snatching up both the Great Guff and Princess Poot and tossing them into the sarcophagus. "I reckon that's just about a small enough space for them to swap gas for a while," he said, kicking the lid closed with his foot.

Luke turned to Cleo. "Aren't you going to lecture him about cruelty to goblins?"

"Normally I would," she replied, glancing at the rapidly approaching ground, "but as we're about to smash into the desert, I'll give it a miss!"

"Smash into the desert?" exclaimed Heru. "Not while I'm here!" He raised his hands and chanted some magic words, and just before it reached the ground the golden chariot screeched to a juddering halt, then rose gently into the air and began to soar around the edge of the pyramid, glinting in the bright sunlight.

Luke, Resus and Cleo gripped the sides and stared at the pharaoh in amazement. He winked at them. "There's no point being a pharaoh if you can't invoke a little mummy magic!"

Meanwhile, the goblins, taking the disappearance of their leader and the sight of a flying

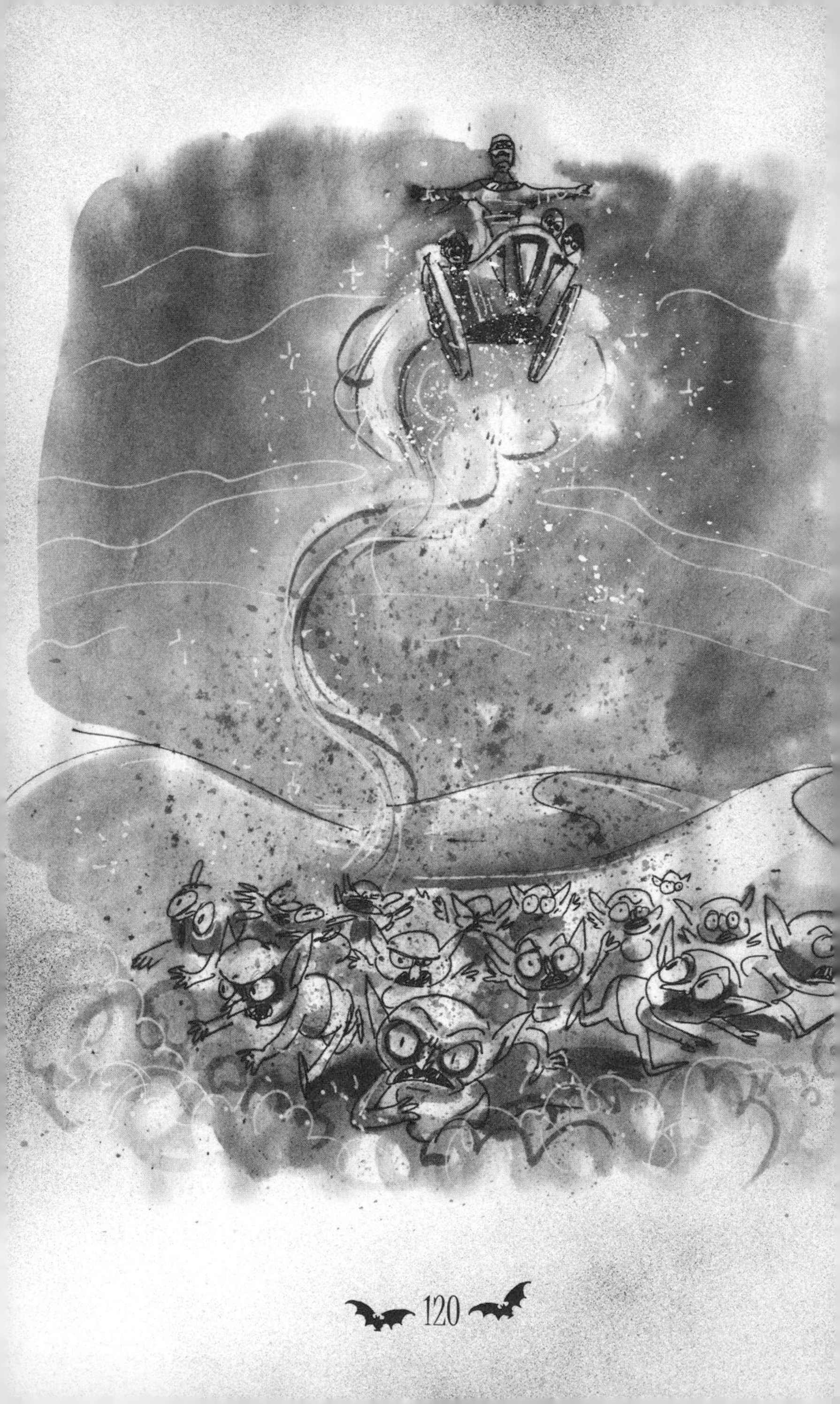

chariot as a sign that their bad day was about to get a lot worse, began to scurry away across the scorching sand. Squiffer raced to keep up with the rest of them, plumes of green gas erupting from his behind.

The chariot finally came to a stop at the base of the pyramid, hovering just above the ground. Then Heru turned one of its golden wheels towards the sun, casting a beam of light onto the side of the stone structure and triggering the secret entrance.

"Remember when we first met Heru and he made us act out his favourite soap opera?" Resus asked in a whisper.

"Like it was yesterday," replied Luke. "Why?"

"Well, I *might* have given the impression that I thought he was nothing but a bandaged buffoon..."

"*Might* have?" spluttered Cleo. "You practically said it to his face!"

"Yeah, well..." grinned Resus. "I take it all back. Egypt's cool – and Heru's the king!"

The pharaoh gestured towards his sarcophagus, which was now floating beside the group. "This is where I leave you," he said, "but I

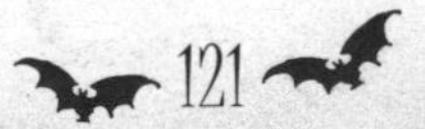

promise to let those two back out once their honeymoon is over."

"You couldn't drop us off at that Hex Hatch before you disappear, could you?" asked Luke.

Heru bowed deeply. "It would be my honour." He muttered another spell and the chariot flew through the air to settle beside the shimmering window.

"There's something we have to do before we go," said Resus. He pulled the heart from his cloak and handed it to Heru.

"This is yours," said Luke. "Thank you so much for the kind gift, and we hope it will help someone else in the future."

"How wonderful!" exclaimed Heru, clutching it tightly. "Just the thing to brighten up that dull, treasure-filled tomb of mine."

Luke turned to Resus and Cleo as they stepped towards the Hex Hatch. "Do you know what I'm most looking forward to about getting back home?" he asked.

Resus shrugged. "Never seeing another mermaid, ever again?"

"Having a sleep without being digested?" suggested Cleo.

Luke grinned. "Both of those, yeah," he said. "But now we've returned another relic, I can't wait to see Sir Otto's face turn the same shade of purple as this Hex Hatch!"

Laughing, the trio jumped into the swirling violet tunnel and headed for home.

Tommy Donbavand was born and brought up in Liverpool and has worked at numerous careers that have included clown, actor, theatre producer, children's entertainer, drama teacher, storyteller and writer. His non-fiction books for children and their parents, *Boredom Busters* and *Quick Fixes for Bored Kids*, have helped him to become a regular guest on radio stations around the UK and he also writes for a number of magazines, including *Creative Steps* and Scholastic's *Junior Education*.

Tommy sees his comedy-horror series *Scream Street* as what might have resulted had Stephen King been the author of *Scooby Doo*. "Writing *Scream Street* is fangtastic fun," he says. "I just have to be careful not to scare myself too much!" Tommy had so much fun writing the first Scream Street books that he decided to set Luke, Resus and Cleo another quest so he'd have an excuse to write some more.

You can find out more about Tommy and his books at his website: www.tommydonbavand.com